THE RESOLUTION

RAVI RANJAN GOSWAMI

Made with ♥ on the Notion Press Platform
www.notionpress.com

Kesha Kumari Goswami, Divita, and Harikrishnan

Contents

Contents

Foreword

The Resolution is a novella featuring common citizens of India and their lives in that era of colonization.

The Quit India Movement was spreading its influence across the country circa 1942. People were ferociously taking part in the independence struggle and were hell-bent on ending the foreign rule on the soil of India. The wave of the movement touched every city and village alike. Despite being trampled by a foreign rule, people had promised resolutions to fulfill and cater to.

This is a story of the dreams and struggles of common people in pre-Independence India; Readers will definitely like this story.

Preface

Pandit Gopinath was the headmaster of the Government Primary School in Konch village. In school, he was sitting in his room looking at the correspondence file. He got worried after reading an administrative letter. Why?

Acknowledgements

I have translated this story from my Hindi Short novel titled Sankalp.

CHAPTER ONE

Pandit Gopinath was the headmaster of the Government Primary School in Konch village. In school, he was sitting in his room looking at the correspondence file. He got worried after reading an administrative letter. The month of May had started and it was getting very hot. That day was the 5th. There was information in the letter that there would be an inspection of the school on the coming 10th and the advice was that all the teaching staff should wear an English dress on that day.

Wearing trousers was a very difficult task for Panditji. He remembered the incident of his marriage. At the time of his marriage, his friends forced him to wear a suit. Somehow, he put on the coat. He stumbled a couple of times while wearing the pants. A friend helped him put on his pants, but he was not able to walk properly. He performed a few important rituals and then switched out the coat and pants for a native dress. A special silk kurta and dhoti were ordered for the wedding.

He was immersed in all these thoughts when Vice Principal Mangal Mishra called from the door, "Can I come in?"

Gopinath said, "Come on, Mishraji. The administration does not fail to show who is ruling us."

Mishraji asked, "Why? What happened?"

Gopinath gave him the file and asked him to read the letter.

Mishraji read the letter and said, "You get nervous quickly. It is only for a day; but a few hours." He had neither problem nor hesitation in wearing a coat and pants.

Mishraji further said to please him, "You will look great in a suit. Inspector Sahib will be happy."

Inspector D'Souza was an Indian but was no less than an Englishman in manners and lifestyle.

Gopinath laughed and asked Mishra, "Is the inspection to be of the school or us?"

Ram Mishra said, "We are part of the school."

Gopinath said, "Okay."

Then a student came and informed them that Gopinath was being called home immediately.

Gopinath became anxious. He handed over the responsibilities of the school to Mishraji and started walking towards his house with quick steps.

CHAPTER TWO

When Gopinath reached home, he saw that his wife was crying. He learned that his eldest son Balkishan had slapped an Englishman in the market.

As the incident was of an Indian slapping an Englishman, the matter was considered serious. The police caught Balkishan and took him to the police station. Gopinath did not understand what to do. But his wife did not let him think much. Crying, she forced him to go to the police station immediately. What had happened was that while he was in the market, Balkishan witnessed a young Englishman beating a cycle rickshaw driver. Balkishan did not know the reason nor did he feel the need to know. All he knew was that the Englishman was beating him badly. Balkishan went and separated the two men and, holding the English man by his collar, gave him eight or ten slaps on both cheeks. The young man ran away shouting something in English. Balkishan came to his house. Balkishan was aware of the seriousness of the incident, so he told his mother that he might be required to go to the police station. The same happened—after a while, Inspector Virendra came with two soldiers and took him to the police station.

Gopinath went to the police station and met Virendra Singh and Balkishan.

The inspector consoled Gopinathji and sent him home, assuring him that Balkishan would be released by the evening. Virendra Singh kept Balkishan sitting in the police station till evening, explaining that there would be trouble if the young man filed a report and Balkishan ran away. However, he heartily appreciated Balkishan's actions. He arranged for food for Balkishan in the police station and got him to write a complaint against that British youth. Had the youth registered a complaint with the police station, a complaint would have been filed on behalf of Balkishan too. However, no complaints were filed.

Public opinion had turned against the British so much that the incident of the beating of a British youth by Balkishan had made Balkishan famous in the surrounding areas. Many villagers congratulated Gopinath for Balkishan's bravery.

Gopinath had two sons. The elder was Balkishan and the younger was Shyamkishan. Being a teacher, he had given special attention to the education of his sons and the result of his efforts was that Balkishan studied till the 10th class. However, after that, Balkishan felt he had fulfilled his duties. He made room in his routine, instead, for working out at the arena in the morning and sleeping early after dinner. Gopinath worked under the light of earthen lamps and candles. He had bought Petromax lanterns for his sons. The younger son had taken advantage of these facilities and graduated from high school with a first division and twelfth with a second division from a school in Orai, a nearby town.

After this incident, Gopinath became concerned for Balkishan's future.

CHAPTER THREE

Balkishan was a 10th class graduate. He was a stout young man with an athletic body. Since Gopinath was becoming worried about his son's future, he thought of getting Balkishan appointed as a primary teacher in his school, a post that was lying vacant.

He told Balkishan his idea.

One day, a few days after the fight with the Englishman, Gopinath said to Balkishan, "There is a vacancy for a primary teacher in my school. You can take the job if you want."

Balkishan said, "But Gandhiji says we need to leave the jobs."

Gopinath said, "That was said during the non-cooperation movement. Now there is no such need."

Balkishan said, “My younger brother has done his twelfth. He is good at studying also. Better get him this job."

Gopinath said, "He will get some job. If you get a job, then I can be carefree.

Balkishan finally said yes.

Giving him Rs 2, Gopinath said, "Get a nice English dress made. Take a tie and learn to tie it too."

Balkishan was happy to get the money for the new dress.

CHAPTER FOUR

Balkishan was sweating, sitting on the bench outside the principal's room of the government school.

D'Souza and Gopinath returned after taking a tour of the school. Balkishan stood looking at them.

D'Souza's attention turned towards him.

Gopinath had not yet spoken to him about Balkishan.

Going inside, D'Souza asked, "Who is the young man standing outside?"

Gopinath said, "Sir, he is my son. I brought him to meet you. He has passed 10th class with good marks. If you are kind, then the boy's life could be made."

D'Souza said, "What can I do?"

Gopinath said, "There is a vacancy for a primary teacher in this school. Please, appoint him on a temporary basis with immediate effect. You can do that. You can make him permanent later."

D'Souza said, "You as the principal can also hire one or two persons if necessary, for temporary roles."

Gopinath said, "I had some hesitation doing this for my son.

D'Souza was sitting on the chair of the principal. Gopinath in front of him. He asked Gopinath to send Balkishan inside.

D'Souza found Balkishan to be extra capable. He could also work as a PT[N1] teacher.

He sent Balkishan out, called Gopinath inside, and said, "Get Balkishan's appointment letter typed and take my signature on it. I will leave after that."

Gopinath ordered the office staff to type the letter.

Gopinath had arranged for food from his home. He himself took out the food from the boxes and served it on plates.

Satisfied with the food, D'Souza left in his car.

There was a festive atmosphere in Gopinath's house that day. However, Balkishan was a little nervous about what and how he would teach.

[N1]As these acronyms might have changed over time, it might be better to give the full form or use a different word.

CHAPTER FIVE

Shyamkishan was good at his studies. He had learned to read, write and type in English. In those days, in government jobs, preference was given to those who knew English. A limited number of candidates were called for appointments. The father of a friend of Shyamkishan was working in the railways in Jhansi. He called Shyamkishan and asked him to apply for the post of clerk in the railways. His sahib was an Englishman whose name was Newman. He interviewed Shyamkishan in which he gave him a one-page dictation in English which Shyamkishan completed well. Shyamkishan got a job in the Railways.

CHAPTER SIX

Landlord Chandrabhan's daughter, Lakshmi, had passed class eight. He was thinking of marrying her off. He had a son Uttam who was older than Lakshmi. He had sent him to the city to study. Lakshmi was a beautiful girl, and in addition to helping her mother with her work, she also learned household work. A few days ago, she had gone to visit Rani Laxmi Bai's fort in Jhansi by horse cart with her parents. Her friend Kala also went with them. They were looking at a cannon named Kadak Bijli kept at a place in the fort, when a handsome young man came and asked with a smile of Kala, "Kala, you are here! With whom have you come?" This young man was Balkishan. He was Kala's cousin.

Kala introduced everyone, "Brother, this is Chandrabhan Tauji, Taiji, and this is my best friend, their daughter Lakshmi."

"This is my brother Balkishan."

Balkishan greeted everyone with folded hands. Laxmi looking at Balkishan with bewilderment, folded both her hands to say namaste. Then they went on their way.

Lakshmi liked Balkishan very much.

Balkishan also liked her. He desired to marry a girl like Lakshmi. A few months later, Balkishan and Lakshmi again came face to face at the wedding of Kala's elder sister.

Their introduction went a little further. But even then, they did not dare to think about marriage. No one knew the future.

Chandrabhan had fixed Lakshmi's marriage with Kundan, the son of a neighboring jagirdar.

Kundan's age was 30 years and Lakshmi's age was about 14 years. The practice of child marriage had not yet been banned completely. According to Kundan, Lakshmi's marriage had been delayed. When Kundan came to see Lakshmi, seeing him, Lakshmi's heart sank. She told her mother about her unwillingness to marry and her mother conveyed her words to Chandrabhan. But Chandrabhan said, "Lakshmi is still ignorant. You explain it to her that this is a good match. Kundan is from a rich family. She will rule in her in-laws' house."

But neither could her mother explain it to Lakshmi nor could Lakshmi explain it to herself. In adolescence, sometimes fantasies seem very real. For no obvious reason, she believed that Balkishan would save her. She knew that the Lady gardener's son often went to Konch. She requested the lady gardener to send a letter to Balkishan at Konch through her son. At first, the lady was afraid so she refused. When Lakshmi requested several times, she agreed. Lakshmi wrote a letter to Balkishan and handed it over to the lady gardener.

The lady gardener gave the letter to her son Lakshmana the next day in a sealed envelope and said, "This is a letter from Lakshmi bhanji. There is a special letter that is to be given to the teacher Balkishan in Konch.

The letter reached Balkishan.

Balkishan had no idea that the matter would reach this point. He discussed the matter with his friend Rafiq.

Rafiq said, "What the landlord's daughter is saying, there seems to be truth in her words."

"You have to do something. There will be no one to stand by her. Who will dare risk enmity with the landlord?"

Balkishan said, "I think I should meet her."

Rafiq said, "Yes, I think the same."

After this discussion, Rafiq returned to his home.

CHAPTER SEVEN

Runaway of Lakshmi

Lakshmi had made up her mind to run away with Balkishan a day before her wedding. There was still conflict in her mind and also the sorrow of leaving her parents and family. Her heart was in her mouth at the thought of her parents becoming sad when they found out that she had run away. She also doubted whether she would ever be able to come home again in the future. Then she controlled her emotions by reminding herself that girls have to go to their in-laws' house after getting married anyway. There were only two options in front of her, to keep everyone happy by marrying a middle-aged man, or to run away from home and marry a groom of her choice. Balkishan's family was also unaware of the coming storm. However, Balkishan was learning horse riding from his friend Rafiq. Rafiq used to drive a tonga. Balkishan was learning horse riding on the horse that used to pull the tonga. The horse sometimes did not understand Balkishan's command. Even after Balkishan would tighten the reins, the horse would take a step forward and stop. They guessed that maybe the horse was feeling lighter and so Balkishan waited for the tonga to be tied to him. Eventually, with constant practice, both the horse and the horse rider started to understand each other. Balkishan also practiced horse riding for a few days by making Rafiq sit behind.

On the night of Vasant Panchami, a thick rope was hanging from the window of Lakshmi, daughter of Jagirdar Chandrabhan. One end of this rope was tied to a leg of the bed kept in the room.

Lakshmi, along with Balkishan, went on a horse to an unknown destination. With great courage, Lakshmi had left a letter in which she had written that due to shame and fear she could not say anything to the family members. She had chosen Balkishan to be her husband, so she was going with him.

CHAPTER EIGHT

Chandrabhan was going mad with anger. Carrying loaded guns, with his men, he searched the surrounding villages and the forests. The girl had gone of her own free will, so he did not make a complaint with the police.

Balkishan came straight to his house with Lakshmi. He got off the horse. Then helped Lakshmi dismount from the horse. She was wearing a red-colored kurta and a white salwar. She was wearing a red scarf. She covered her head with a scarf before facing Balkishan's mother as a mark of respect.

The door was closed. Balkishan knocked on the door. Sarla, his mother, opened the door. Seeing the girl with Balkishan, she got thinking. The girl bent and touched her feet.

Sarla asked Balkishan, "Who is this girl?"

He narrated the whole story and said, "Now she is in your refuge. Both of us are in your refuge. We will do as you command."

His mother held Lakshmi's hand and said, "I take her in my shelter. You have to fight your own battle." Saying this she took Lakshmi inside the house with her."

Balkishan stood in a state of distrust for a while. Then, he went to his room.

CHAPTER NINE

The name of the English officer who had hired Shyamkishan was Newman. He was an engineer.

He was so impressed with Shyamkishan that he made him his secretary. Shyamkishan was also happy with Newman.

What made Shyamkishan happy was that Newman sahib did not seem English. Tales of the bitter mood of the British officers were common. However, Newman had lived in India for ten years and, after living in Kanpur for five years, he had come to Jhansi on a transfer. Moreover, he knew Hindi.

CHAPTER TEN

City

Newman assured Shyamkishan he would get a house in the Railway Colony. But the colony was far from the city. Shyamkishan liked living in the city more among the markets, hotels, and so on. There were also more facilities in the city. In the atmosphere of that time, people were filled with the impatient desire for freedom, opposition towards the British, and the spirit of sacrifice, especially sacrifice for freedom. Shyamkishan would hesitate to talk about his job. If the neighbors talked about something, he would think they were only discussing him. Therefore, when Master Sahib, a revolutionary and social worker, proposed to hold a secret meeting of the revolutionaries at his residence, he accepted. Such meetings used to move from place to place. There was always the threat of police raids. Shyamkishan's house was suitable for the meeting. One, he used to live there alone in those days; second, he was a government servant. The police was less likely to suspect him.

Shyamkishan thought that it would be a meeting of some small local leaders. But then, he came to know that his area was very active in the freedom struggle. The meeting of revolutionaries held at his residence restored his self-respect.

Master Sahib also told him, "War is fought on many fronts at many levels. You are also a soldier of freedom."

CHAPTER ELEVEN

The people of Konch village and the surrounding areas started seeing Balkishan as a revolutionary. The people of the enlightened class and revolutionaries of the area started inviting him to their meetings. Seeing the attitude and faith of all the people towards him, Balkishan made up his mind to leave his government job. He discussed this matter with the members of the house. Nobody objected. Gopinath expressed his concern about how the household expenses would be met after he left the job. It was expected that expenses would increase in the future.

Balkishan had thought about this matter.

One day, when Gopinath asked Balkishan, "What will you do after leaving the job?"

Balkishan said, "I will teach the children at home."

Gopinath was pleased to hear this.

CHAPTER TWELVE

When Chandrabhan came to know that Lakshmi had gone with a young man named Balkishan and that the young man was the son of Gopinathji of Konchgram, his worries were over. Gopinathji was a distinguished dignitary of the village and the surrounding areas. Gopinath himself had sent the news of Lakshmi's coming with Balkishan to Chandrabhan. Along with this, he had also proposed to get Balkishan and Lakshmi married, which Chandrabhan gladly accepted. This was the period when people were fighting for the Independence of India. The Indian National Congress launched the Quit India Movement in August 1942 at the Bombay session of the Congress Committee under the leadership of Mahatma Gandhi.

Balkishan left the job on the call of Gandhiji. Nevertheless, Chandrabhan got his daughter Lakshmi duly married to Balkishan and sent his daughter away from the house in a palanquin. Balkishan started tutoring the children at home.

This topic was also discussed with Shyamkishan. He was able to help the local revolutionary groups more by continuing his job. However, he too could not stay on at his job for long.

CHAPTER THIRTEEN

The anti-British wave was overflowing in India. Many people had resigned from government jobs. The atmosphere had become very bad for the British. At times, lonely Englishmen could be seen being teased and driven away by the local boys in isolated areas. Shyamkishan could not hate Neuman. He never abused or tortured anyone. He did not deviate from his courteous manners, even while talking to his juniors and subordinates.

In his Quit India speech, Gandhi asked all Indians, including teachers, to quit their jobs and participate in the movement. Shyamkishan thought that the British from the political ruling class needed to leave India, not people like Newman.

But when he saw a group of youths shouting "British leave India" in front of Newman's house, he became concerned. Newman and his wife decided to leave India because they perhaps were starting to feel unsafe. They were also being missed by their children and grandchildren living in London.

Shyamkishan made sure that Newman and his family were able to safely leave Jhansi.

He escorted them to the railway station and boarded them on a night train to Bombay. The next day, Shyamkishan resigned from his job.

Shyamkishan along with his father opened a small printing press and started a Hindi daily newspaper.

When some marriage proposals came for Shyamkishan, he politely declined. He had decided that he would marry only when the country became Independent. Everyone respected his decision. Knowing his decision, without informing anyone, a bachelorette from the neighborhood decided that she would wait for the country to become Independent and then marry Shyamkishan.

Everyone wanted and was waiting for the Independence of the country.

CHAPTER FOURTEEN

The girl who thought of marrying Shyamkishan after Independence was Lali, the 17-year-old daughter of a neighboring confectioner, Rajjan Seth. At first, he thought that she would not tell anyone, but one day when Subhadra came to meet her, she could not stop herself and told Subhadra what was on her mind.

Subhadra kept looking at her stunned. Lali asked her, "Why are you looking at me like that?"

Subhadra said, "Have you lost your mind? You have never even talked with Shyamkishan in this regard. And you took such a vow? What if his parents fix his marriage somewhere else?"

Lali said without hesitation, "If Balkishan can get married according to his wish, that too by kidnapping a girl, then it can happen with Shyamkishan also."

Subhadra asked, "And if Shyamkishan likes some other girl?"

Lali said seriously, "If I can't become Radha, I will become Meera."

Talks of Subhadra's marriage were going on. She felt sorry for Lali. She was worried about whom Lali would confide in once she went to her in-laws' house. She knew that Lali had no other friend as close as her.

She remained with Lali for about an hour, then took her to leave and went home.

That evening, she prayed for the fulfillment of Lali's oath.

CHAPTER FIFTEEN

Political Ideology

There was no clear ideology subscribed to by Gopinath and his family. He considered the Independence of India his sacred goal, be it through the effort of any political party or social organization. Whoever worked in the interest of the country got a proper place in Gopinath's newspaper "Karmayogi". Shyamkishan had liked the Communist Party during his stay in Jhansi. But he was an admirer of Gandhi. He was greatly influenced by the personality and lifestyle of the Mahatma. Shyamkishan had also participated in a couple of communist meetings. But he did not understand the opposition to the Quit India Movement by the Communist Party of India. He was disillusioned with that party.

Balkishan was filled with enthusiasm after reading the tales of revolutionaries. However, he felt like he was not doing anything for the country.

Every morning while drinking tea, he would quietly say to Lakshmi so as not to be overheard by Gopinathji, "I am thinking of serving my country service by joining some organization or party."

Lakshmi said, "As you wish. But according to me, you don't need a special party or platform to serve the country. Whoever performs all his duties properly serves the country."

Balkishan said, "That is also true."

Then the children would come and Balkishan would get busy teaching them.

CHAPTER SIXTEEN

Shyamkishan's Sister

Subhadra treated Shyamkishan as her brother. After returning from Lali's house to her home, she kept thinking about her while lying in bed that night. Not only did she want to convey Lali's thoughts to Shyamkishan, but she also wanted to prepare him to marry Lali. She was feeling scared. There must not be anyone else in Shyamkishan's mind. She knew that he used to work in the railways. There he was in the company of the British. What if he had fallen into the trap of a blonde? She shuddered at this thought. She shrugged off the idea. She consoled herself that she would have heard about such a thing. If there was a fire, there would have been smoke. She decided to do something quickly in this matter.

It seemed that Subhadra was more concerned about Lali than her parents. The next morning, she reached Lali's house.

She found Lali's mother sitting on the ground in the

CHAPTER SEVENTEEN

Lali

More than Lali, her mother was interested in her dress and make-up. In her opinion, Lali was of marriageable age, so she needed to be a little groomed so that she had a good image in society and within the community. She asked Lali to wear a pink georgette saree. She made her hair too. When Lali saw the mirror, she praised her mother in her heart. She only wore slippers. She found slippers most comfortable to walk in.

When she reached Subhadra's house, Subhadra's mother praised her saying she looked beautiful and she became shy.

At Subhadra's behest, both of them went to the temple that day by cycle rickshaw. Subhadra did not want to turn gray with dust before reaching the temple.

There was a crowd of people at the well outside the temple. Everyone used to wash their hands and feet before entering the temple. Some youths were washing the hands and feet of visitors by drawing water from the well using a bucket. Subhadra and Lali took off their slippers and washed their hands and feet and entered the temple. The courtyard of the temple was very big. Fruit trees were planted on the sides under which stone benches were made to sit. There was a huge crowd in the temple. Subhadra's eyes were searching for someone in the crowd. Subhadra knew that Shyamkishan visited the temple of Goddess

Bhavani almost every Friday. Finally, she spotted Shyamkishan sitting on a bench in the courtyard. She grabbed Lali's hand and moved towards Shyamkishan. Lali blushed upon seeing Shyamkishan and tried to stop Subhadra. But Subhadra almost dragged her to Shyamkishan.

Going closer to Shyamkishan, she said, "Hello brother."

Shyamkishan glanced at Lali, then looked at Subhadra and said, "Namaste."

He asked, "Has mother also come?"

Subhadra said, "No. We both have come."

Then, she introduced Lali. "This is my friend Lali, who lives in your neighborhood."

Shyamkishan jokingly said, "That's great. My neighbor is being introduced to me by you.

Subhadra asked, "Do you recognize her?"

Shyamkishan said, "She is Kachori uncle's daughter. You just told me the name, Lali."

Subhadra said, "You are the hidden Rustam."

Shyamkishan said, "Hey, neighbors must have this much information at least."

"Am I correct Lali?" Shyamkishan asked Lali to include her in the conversation.

Lali said, "Yes."

Subhadra said to Shyamkishan, "Today you have to go back with us."

Shyamkishan asked, "Why? Any special reason?"

Subhadra said, "We want to go after seeing the aarti of the Goddess. But it will be dark by then."

Shyamkishan said, "I too have stopped for the aarti. We will go together." Lali felt shy, but she was happy too. She could not understand whether it was coincidence or planning. Subhadra did not tell her anything about

Shyamkishan meeting them at the temple.

After the aarti, all three of them went on foot to the house. Even if they wanted to go by rickshaw or tonga, they would have had to walk some distance by foot because they would have been able to find tongas only after reaching the road.

While walking, Shyamkishan asked Subhadra, "Does Lali study?"

“It is only possible to study up to class 8 here, so both of us have completed it. After that, she learned sewing and weaving at home. Lali also makes sweets. Sometimes she makes sweets in the shop."

Lali was walking silently.

Shyamkishan asks Lali to join the conversation, “Lali, you are very quiet.”

Lali replied naively “No one is talking to me at all."

All three of them started laughing at this.

Subhadra said, "Let me tell you one more thing about her. She writes poems too."

Shyamkishan became more interested in this matter.

He said to Lali, “That’s very good. Show me one or two of your poems. If possible, I will publish them in the weekly appendix of my daily paper.”

Subhadra was happy. She said excitedly, “Brother, when you print the poem, definitely send me a copy of that issue.”

Talking along the way, they didn’t realize when they reached their houses. It was quite dark and the street lamps were lit. Shyamkishan and Subhadra first dropped Lali to her house. Lali’s mother was anxiously standing at the door. She was relieved to see Subhadra and Shyamkishan together with Lali.

After that, Shyamkishan dropped Subhadra at her house and then went to his own house.

When Shyamkishan reached home, everyone had gone to sleep after having dinner. Mother was awake. When he knocked on the door, mother asked, "Who is it?"

Shyamkishan said, "I am Shyam."

Mother opened the door. A lantern was burning in the courtyard. His mother raised its flame. It started burning a little brighter.

Mother laid a mat near the lantern and said to Shyamkishan, "Sit down. I'll serve food."

Shyamkishan washed his hands and feet and sat on the mat. The light of the lantern was reaching the kitchen. Mother brought a serving plate from the kitchen.

After having dinner, he went to his room and sat at his table and lit a candle. In its light, he wrote some points to be included in the next editorial, then slept on the cot.

CHAPTER EIGHTEEN

Shyamkishan's meeting with Lali had had an effect. In the editorial section of the next edition of the "Karmayogi" newspaper, Shyamkishan penned an excellent article on women's education. In it, he stressed the need to open schools in the village that provided education up till class 12. And in the Sunday special issue, he gave a special place to the literary works of local women. A children's poem by Lali was published. Lali and Subhadra had a big hand in the compilation of these works. The families of many of these women composers were unaware of their talent. Most people expressed surprise and appreciation. Some people got angry. When Lali's father came to know about her poetic talent, he was happy. He was fond of Urdu poetry. And despite being less educated, he remembered the fifty verses of Ghalib. Through the initiative of Shyamkishan, a committee of six people from the village was formed whose responsibility was to work for the development of education in the village. Gopinath was made its chief. As a result of the efforts of this committee, the foundation of a higher secondary school for boys and girls was laid within a year. Seth Kedar, a wealthy villager, donated land for this work. The school would be completed in the next two years.

CHAPTER NINETEEN

Nearly a year had passed since Subhadra's marriage had been fixed. The Muhurta for the marriage was on June 15 of that summer. Subhadra's in-laws' house was in Orai, which was not far away, but Subhadra felt that she was going too far. Subhadra's groom, Chandu, had opened a grocery shop. He was good looking. She was satisfied with this. Three or four days before the wedding, the whole village was busy with the preparations for the wedding. Every person was involved in the preparations as if it were their own sister or daughter who was getting married. Shyamkishan was entrusted with the care of the reception and lodging of the marriage party. Lali took charge of Subhadra's clothes and costumes. Lali's father made all the arrangements for the food for the bride's side and the bridegroom's side. For this, two or three big earthen stoves were prepared in the courtyard of Subhadra's house.

After all this, the day finally arrived when Chandu came to Subhadra's house on a mare with a procession and the marriage was solemnized after they took the customary seven rounds around the holy fire. All the wedding rituals took place at night.

Preparations for the farewell went on all of the next morning.

Subhadra was restless. She called Shyamkishan.

As Shyamkishan was like her brother, she did not hesitate to call him into the room and talk in private.

She said to Shyamkishan, “I have called to tell you a something special."

Shyamkishan said, "Tell me, what is the matter?"

Subhadra looked at Shyamkishan with tearful eyes and said, "You have taken an oath to get married only when the country becomes Independent, haven’t you?"

Shyamkishan said, "Yes, but why are you so upset?”

Subhadra said, “My dear friend has decided not to get married like you till the country becomes Independent.”

Shyamkishan guessed and asked, "Who? Is it Lali?"

Subhadra said, "Yes."

Shyamkishan exclaimed, "Oh!"

Subhadra said, "You don’t even know! That crazy girl has decided that she will marry you then."

Then Lali entered the room. She greeted Shyamkishan and said to Subhadra, “Everyone is waiting for you at the door. Let us go.”

Subhadra, sobbing and hugging Shyamkishan, said softly, "Brother, take care of her."

Then Subhadra and Lali hugged and started crying. Then the voice of Subhadra’s father came, "Somebody call Subhadra. The time for the farewell is passing."

Lali held Subhadra’s hand and took her outside. Shyamkishan also came out behind them.

Subhadra bid a final farewell with tearful eyes after saying goodbye to all the family members. She went to her in-laws’ house in the bus with her groom. She left the void of her absence.

It took a couple of days for the sadness to go away from the village.

CHAPTER TWENTY

The "Karmayogi" newspaper had given women an excellent platform for expression. Many girls including Lali had enrolled for further studies in the newly opened higher secondary school. Highly educated teachers came from other places and settled there. This brought a significant change to the educational and social structure of the village.

Navratri was close.

Gopinath, Kedar, Rajan Halwai, the music teacher Bhatnagar and some other members were present in this time's Ram Leela committee meeting. Gopinath said, "This time, it would be better if a young man is made to act as Hanuman in my place."

Kedar said, "No one can do a better Hanuman than you."

Gopinath said, "If you give them the opportunity, it will happen."

Bhatnagar said, "We should take the work of female characters from male actors. If a woman is willing to act, at least we can keep her for the role of Sita. The level of the Leela will rise further."

A couple of people opposed this.

However, Seth Kedar agreed, "There is weight in what Master Saab is saying. There is a reason as well. It will be good if we can do this for at least a couple of acts. This year, the district collector who is coming is a Hindustani, Ankur Banerjee. He has talked about organizing a Ram

Leela competition for the district."

Hearing this, people got excited and unanimously passed a resolution that this time a girl would be chosen for the role of Sita.

Master Bhatnagar would select the characters for Ram Leela. Gopinathji would play Hanuman this time as well.

CHAPTER TWENTY-ONE

and Sita

One doesn't know if it was providence or a coincidence. Master Bhatnagar had seen Shyamkishan and Lali at Subhadra's wedding and had thought to himself that if they became a pair, they would look like the pair—Ram and Sita. On getting the responsibility of selecting the actors for the Ram Leela, the master persuaded Shyamkishan and Lali and their family members that they should act in the Ram Leela.

When the Ram Leela was staged, Shyamkishan initially felt some hesitation to act in front of his father. However, he soon took control of himself.

The Sita and Ram pair became a hit. The collector declared their Ram Leela the winner.

CHAPTER TWENTY-TWO

Whenever there was talk about Lali's marriage in Lali's house, she would make excuses.

Her family members could not understand why Lali wanted to postpone her marriage.

Perhaps Lali's family members would have gotten her married then, but the planet Mars helped her.

Lali was Manglik according to her birth chart, that is, Mars was full of defects in her horoscope. According to astrology, only a Manglik groom would be suitable for her. However, such a groom was not to be found soon. Meanwhile, a conversation started between Lali and Shyamkishan. Both of them had come closer than before.

Time passed. The sacrifice and struggle of the people of India, leaders and countless revolutionaries paid off. The day of India's Independence had been decided. India became Independent on 15 August 1947. Unprecedented celebrations erupted all over India. Konch village was also beautifully decorated. Gold merchants decorated the jewelry bazaar with gold and silver jewelry.

Subhadra came to her maternal home for this joyous gaiety.

Seeing this as the right time, she told Lali's parents about Lali's oath and recommended she marry Shyamkishan. They asked the priest of the family about the Manglik dosha in the horoscope, and he was also in favor of Lali's marriage to Shyamkishan.

Lali's parents went to Gopinath's house and proposed the marriage of Lali and Shyamkishan, which was accepted. Subhadra had already told them about Lali's oath and her devotion to Shyamkishan.

Lali and Shyamkishan were married on the 16 August 1947. The special thing about this marriage was that this was performed under the protection of the tricolor—the Indian flag was flying above the wedding stage. The resolutions of both Lali and Shyamkishan were fulfilled.

Ravi Ranjan Goswami is a master of science by academics. He is retired from Indian Revenue Service. He is fond of reading and writing poetry, some of his published books are dialogue poetry collection, my five stories, The Gold Syndicate (Novel), Looteron Ka Tila Chambal (a short novel), Hindi romance novel Samantar Prem, Sankalp (short Hindi novel).

9 798887 042602

Printed by Libri Plureos GmbH in Hamburg,
Germany